I0534026

SWAMP WITCH

By: Ricardo S. Dubois

Edited: Angela Hooper

Back Photo: Courtesy of Dwight Moore

SWAMP WITCH

SWAMP WITCH

Lill Tee watched, as his mama moved about the kitchen, oblivious to his presence. It was a morning ritual that had been repeated hundreds of times before. She moved about the kitchen with measured, deliberate movements that enabled her to complete her tasks in the most efficient manner possible. Through the years, she had been able to establish a routine that just seemed to work for her.

Mama was a slender shapely woman, who had been able to maintain her striking looks despite the hardships and rigors of daily life. Her blond hair, only now starting to show signs of graying, was still an unusual sight in an area dominated by a French heritage that produced brown hair, brown-eyed offspring. Lill Tee's mama, however, did not trace her ancestry to France of Nova Scotia like most Cajuns. Her father had immigrated to Louisiana from Germany, a people whose physical characteristics are remarkably different. Sought out by many would be suitors, it was Lill Tee's papa who would ultimately claim her for his own.

As Lill Tee continued to watch his mama move about the kitchen, he noticed a small trace of smoke, slowly crawling out of the hearth. Curious to its ultimate destination, Lill Tee followed its movement, as it swirled to and fro as though following some unseen trail. Lill Tee had seen plenty of smoke in his life, yet for some reason, this particular smoke had captured his imagination. He watched as the single band of smoke separated into two, weakening its white trail to a hazy mist as it continued to meander up the wall and onto the ceiling. Meeting up with smoke that had arrived some time earlier, a contest of sorts ensued.

As the cooler smoke met the warmer smoke, they coiled and swirled about. Like two sumo wrestlers, they competed for dominance, selfishly guarding every inch of their territory until finally the dominator would submit its opponent to its will, only to be dominated by a newer stronger force that followed immediately behind.

The lingering traces of smoke, which slowly swirled about the small kitchen ceiling, formed a Kaleidoscope of movement, ever-changing as it swirled about searching for the elusive way out of the cabin. The escape for most of the smoke, however, would be to permeate the already smoke-saturated cypress ceiling beams, or layer itself on top of previous smoke, giving the beams an even older rustic look.

Normally, Lill Tee was still asleep during this time of early morning. He had never seen first hand how hard she worked at preparing the meals. Only now did he begin to appreciate how much work went into preparing what he thought was a simple breakfast. All Lill Tee ever saw was the end result. After today, he would walk away with a greater appreciation of what his mother had to do in the early morning when they were all still asleep.

Not having any of the modern conveniences

that had emerged at the turn of the century, Lill Tee and his family lived like his ancestors had lived for generations .... off the land.

A land teaming with wildlife, and enough raw material to sustain them through the hardest of times.

Lill Tee's mama poked at the firewood in the hearth, summoning forth new flames to complete her task. Lill Tee began to recall the hours he had spent laying in front of the fireplace. The duel purpose opening provided both warmth in the winter, and fire on which to cook and bake the delicious meals Lill Tee had taken for granted.

The aroma of the freshly baked biscuits brought his senses to full alert as his nose signaled the brain, who in turn awoke his stomach to the anticipation of what was to come.

The family lived in a large two-bedroom cabin complete with a loft, built on one of the few hills in the area, with wood cut and honed from cypress taken from the swamp. The cabin was built with the blood and sweat of Papa and Mama's hard work. Strategically located among numerous large oak trees, most well over a hundred years old. The location of the cabin was well thought-out by his father, taking into consideration the harshness of the seasons. The large overhanging branches provided protection from the scorching hot Louisiana summers, and also served as a wind break for the piecing winter winds that would sometimes find their way south. From their front porch the family could look down upon a picturesque scene of their brown bayou, which meandered its way through the cypress swamp, an area they called home.

"Why you up so early?" questioned Lill Tee's mama, as though he had just arrived.

"Don't know?" Lill Tee responded, somewhat surprised that she had been so totally engrossed in her work she had completely overlooked him.

"I just woke up early," Lill Tee said, not

bothering to mention how long he had been here.

"How bout Cotile?" Mama asked, referring to Lill Tee's little sister, four years younger.

"She's still asleep. I'll go get her up for you," Lill Tee volunteered. "Must have been pretty tired."

"Must have," Mama agreed. "You leave her be," Mama said, then went back to her cooking.

Lill Tee noticed a half filled bowl of figs on the table. August was normally a very productive harvest, with bowls and bowls of figs on the table. This season, however, was not. The area was hit with a devastating frost the year before, destroying most of the trees and severely curtailing the yield on the remaining survivors.

"Figs didn't produce well this year," said Lill Tee, reporting his observation of the harvest. Lill Tee did not participate in the harvesting and canning of the figs. According to his papa, that was woman's work, and was reserved for his mama and little sister Cotile. Mama had apparently long since accepted this role, but as

SWAMP WITCH

for Cotile, she resisted it with every waking breath. Though his sister would complain, not about the work, but about not being able to do more. She often would ask Papa to go hunting and trapping. You could see Papa's heart ache when she asked, but deep down he knew in the nineteen thirties, there weren't very many opportunities for women with the spirit Cotile had. It would take several more generations for girls like Cotile to realize their full potential. As vocal as his little sister was, Lill Tee could never remember a moment his mama ever complained or seemed anything other than happy. It was as though she accepted her role in life and found happiness everywhere she went.

Though somewhat sheltered from the outside world, Lill Tee was not totally unaware of what was happening in the rest of the world. He had heard folks say a Great Depression had consumed the country and the world. But Lill Tee and his family were so poor already, they had hardly noticed.

SWAMP WITCH

Lill Tee could not look at the bowl of figs without thinking about his mother. The joy in her face when she would peel a plump juicy fig. Pleasures were few in the swamp and so were smiles. So when Lill Tee saw his parents smile, he usually remembered.

"Mama's birthday is coming up soon," Lill Tee thought, he thought about what he could make that would bring that elusive smile to her face. Money to buy things like presents was scarce, and usually saved to purchase things like rice and flour, things they could not readily harvest from the swamp.

As far as meals went, Lill Tee could not remember a single time he had gone hungry. His papa usually always could kill a dear or rabbit to serve up at mealtime.

Little Tee looked at the partially filled bowl of figs. Then as though a light somehow went off in his head, he knew what he was going to get Mama for her birthday! "Figs!" But not just any figs, these would be special. He had heard stories

SWAMP WITCH

of a place where figs grew the size of your fist. Figs Mama would love, and surely bring a smile to her face. The only problem was, it was in the garden of the Swamp Witch!

The Swamp Witch, as she was known among the children of the bayou, lived deep in the swamp in an area where no one dared to venture into. Some folks say the whole area was cursed, and they stayed clear whenever possible.

Chock-a-block full of apples, oranges, and gigantic fig trees. Lill Tee could not think of a better gift than to give his mama a sack of big, juicy figs.

The danger, however, was evident. If he got caught! Well, stories in the swamp abound, and many are about people who venture into the swamp, never to be seen again.

Lill Tee had been told stories of the Swamp Witch since he was a small child. It scared him then and the thought scared him now. Stories like the Swamp Witch could cast a spell on you that would make you just a few inches tall. Then she would keep you as pet if you were lucky. If your luck wasn't so good, you were eaten on the spot. Stories were told that she had gray hair, long fingernails, warts and fang-like teeth. She is said to live in a house made of human bones and pathways lined with teeth of her many victims.

Hearing stories like this, it's no wonder why Cajun boys and girls were so fearful to wander too far from home. One could also conclude that maybe that's why they were told the stories. One thing was certain, no one had ever told Lill Tee it wasn't true.

Hearing the door to his parents' room open, Lill Tee turned to see Papa coming out of his bedroom, the only other room in the house. Papa was at best considered an average size man as Cajuns went. Five foot eight and two hundred pounds, Papa had always been plenty big enough to accomplish whatever he set his mind to. Papa was only thirty-eight years old, but to look at him, you would think he was much older.

The hard life he had lived left their scars,

not only in his memories, but also in the wrinkles and scarred lines that were displayed prominently on his unshaven face. Fully dressed in overalls and a Tee shirt, Papa pulled out a chair and sat next to Lill Tee.

"Good Morning, Papa," said Lill Tee, as he sipped his cup of milk, not waiting for response.

"Good morning son!" Papa responded, in his broken French dialect. "How's my Lill Swamp Rat doing today?" he asked, referring to the nickname he had given Lill Tee.

"Fine, Papa, what are we going to do today?" Lill Tee asked, curious about the day's activity.

When you survived off the land, much of your time was devoted to hunting, and scouting new areas to hunt. Each day it seemed was different, but Lill Tee didn't seem to mind He loved hunting with his papa and learning the lessons only a father could pass on to his son.

"We're going to check our crawfish traps," Papa said, waiting for Lill Tee's response.

SWAMP WITCH

Lill Tee's eyes lit up; there was nothing in this world Lill Tee loved more than crawfish.

"Oh boy!" Lill Tee exclaimed, just as his Little sister Cotile was coming down the stairs.

Cotile was a miniature version of her mom, blonde hair, with blue eyes. Cotile was a developing beauty that would no doubt capture the heart of many young Cajun in the not so distance future.

"Oh boy what?" Cotile asked, not sure what the excitement was about.

"Your brother and I are going to check our crawfish traps," Papa said, explaining Lill Tee's excitement. "If everything goes alright, we should have us a nice feast tonight."

Papa knew what was coming next; it was the same request he had heard so many times before. The pleas that would tear his hardened old heart to pieces.

"Can I go, Papa? Can I?" Cotile pleaded, "I can be a lot of help to you and Lill Tee, I'm strong, I can work hard," Cotile said, making an argument for her to be allowed to go.

Papa had heard the arguments before, he loved his daughter so much, but he knew being a swamp rat was not what was going to serve her well in the future. She would have to learn from Mama how to be a future wife.

"I'm sorry little one," Papa began to explain. "Your mama needs you here."

"But Papa!" Cotile began to protest, knowing the end result before she began.

"Now Cotile," Mama joined in. "What kind of wife you gonna make if you don't learn how to cook and bake."

"I don't want to be a wife!" Cotile protested, "I want to be a trapper like Papa!"

Papa and Mama disregarded the statement as pure fantasy. After all, this was the nineteen thirties and women, especially Cajun women, were for the most part, pigeon-holed into their roles in life. Get married, raise a family, cook, clean and sew. Careers were virtually unheard of for young women.

SWAMP WITCH

Lill Tee felt sorry for Cotile, seeing her desire to break the mold that was placed on her by the previous generation. As few as Lill Tee's options in life were, he still had considerably more than Cotile.

Cotile slowly conceded her inevitable fate for the moment, and they all sat down for a hearty breakfast. Fresh biscuits piping hot from the Dutch oven, topped with homemade molasses with fresh buttermilk. Occasionally, they would have bacon, but because Papa did not raise hogs, he had to trade for it or buy it, and it was so expensive, it was an exception not the rule.

Once in a while, Papa would trade for a hog, which was butchered. Because of the lack of refrigeration, not to mention electricity, meat had to be salted in a barrel to preserve it. This was done by placing a layer of salt then a layer of meat, continuing the process until the entire portion of meat was layered between salt. Then a heavy solution of brine water was poured over the contents then covered. This would preserve the meat for later use.

After breakfast was completed, Lill Tee gathered their few belonging, preparing to embark on their journey. Papa and Lill Tee headed out the house and down the wooden plank to their skiff.

Looking over their shoulder, Lill Tee and Papa waved goodbye to Cotile and Mama, who had come out on the porch to see them off.

Lill Tee placed the sack his mama had given him into the skiff and climbed in, joining his papa, who was already aboard.

The skiff was a flat-bottomed boat propelled by oars, low off the water and only four feet wide and twelve feet long. The skiff offered plenty of space for cargo of all sorts, whether transporting animals Papa had trapped, or a large area to hold crawfish for sacking, the large open area front provided a universal holding area.

"Push us off son," Papa said, as Lill Tee complied, leaning against the piling, pushing the skiff away from the dock so Papa could start oaring.

Lill Tee watched his sister and mama on the porch until the skiff rounded a small bend in the bayou and they disappeared out of sight.

As Papa's oars rippled, they started easing their way toward the bank. The bayou was dead calm, and with the exception of the turbulence from the boat, the water took on appearance of glass. The sun had not yet risen; only the orange glow of its promise could be seen to the east. The moon, however, lingered behind, as though defiant of the chasing sun. Casting light on the brown bayou water, the moon illuminated the reflection of the trees and wildlife along the bayou.

Papa did not row long before they arrived at their first trap. Pulling up next to an overhanging branch, which served as an anchor for the trap, Papa began to pull on the small rope he had anchored to the branch days before. Within a few moments, a wire mesh net appeared, full of the luscious mudbugs they craved.

"Crawfish!" Lill Tee screamed, not being able to contain his excitement. "Wow! Look at the size of the bugs," he exclaimed, noting the bigger than usual tails.

"Yea," Papa replied, "they're nice all right, we do this good on every net, we might be able to trade some."

Barter was a primary means of obtaining the goods and services needed, since money was so scarce. Folks would often complain and moan about the depression, but things had not changed in their life in the least. They did not eat any more or less, and were just as happy.

Net after net Lill Tee and his papa checked, located from the mental map etched into Papa's memory. It had proved to be a substantial harvest with plenty of extra, which made Lill Tee's papa exceptionally happy.

Up until this point, he did not know what he was going to do for Mama's birthday. The harvest Papa had hoped for came true. Now he could trade some Crawfish for a present for Mama's birthday. Things had worked out just fine. They would have all the crawfish they could eat plus Papa could trade for Mama's gift.

As they headed back, the sun had long since made its presence known. Its warming rays were welcomed, as the sun totally illuminated Lill Tee's world.

Brown bayou water slowly gliding its way along the canopy of cypress and oaks, which lined the bank holding the bayou on course with an almost undetectable current. Cypress trees draped with Spanish moss competed with each other for the sun, each stretching a little higher until they loomed over the bayou like rockets ready to be launched. Egrets were spaced out along the bank starting the ritual of foraging the banks for food. Their awkward and lanky appearance could not easily be unnoticed, with a neck that extended almost twice the length of their body. Although an oddity on land, one could not help but to marvel when they witnessed their graceful flight. The banks of the bayou were teaming with wildlife such as deer, raccoon, otters, and muskrat, just to name a few. Each and every one calling the bayou home, each taking just what they needed to survive. Just as the entire bayou inhabitants did. As Papa rowed the skiff, Lill Tee began to sack the crawfish into burlap bags about a foot and a half wide and three feet high, the sacks were too heavy for him to handle after they were full, but presented no problem for him to fill them.

"Finish that sack, Lill Tee," Papa said. "We'll drop it off at Tee John's. We don't want your mama to suspect something's up, before she'll get surprised."

"Sure, Papa," Lill Tee responded, clearly excited and delighted for another reason he had not disclosed to his Papa. "This will give me an opportunity to talk Jean Paul into coming with me when I go after figs!" Lill Tee thought, as he continued to sack the crawfish. "I'm not quite sure what I'm going to face when I venture into the Swamp Witch domain," Lill Tee continued to ponder any unforeseen eventualities that may arise. "I might need a little help, and if the stories are any indication to what lies ahead," Lill Tee's thoughts were interrupted as Papa eased the craft next to the dock.

"Grab the piling," Papa said as Lill Tee moved to the front of the boat.

Lill Tee grabbed the first pilling on the dock and walked it down the boat until his papa had a hand on it, then he returned to the front of the boat to secure the bow. Within a few seconds, working together Lill Tee and Papa had the boat secured.

Tee John and Jean Paul were outside working on fishing nets, which was normally the case. Jean Paul's daddy was a Hoop Net fisherman, and occupied much of his time either repairing or building new nets.

Hoop nets are tubular nets which are held extended by a pole on the front and back inside, the net is expanded with rings that opens the net allowing fish to swim into the funnel-shaped net and trap them in the rear. Jean Paul's dad fished, his sons helped for the most part until it was determined they were old enough to help and not be a hindrance to the process.

This free time that both Jean Paul and Lill Tee enjoyed was usually spent together in pursuit of adventures of some kind. Jean Paul and Lill Tee had been friends as long as they could remember. They were always off fishing, hunting, or just exploring.

Unlike Lill Tee, who was slightly built with brown hair, and a dark completion, Jean Paul was a plump lad with a heart proportional to his size. They were both the same age, twelve, but because of Jean Paul's size, he was often mistaken for being older. A true and loyal friend, Jean Paul had always been there for Lill Tee. He could always count on Jean Paul.

"Jean," Tee John, called out, referring to Papa's real name. "What you up to?" he asked, as he walked up to Lill Tee and Papa, who was just getting out of the skiff.

"Lill Tee and me were checking traps this morning", Papa answered, knowing his response was more rhetorical, since the day's catch was in plain sight in front of the boat.

"How did you do?" Tee John, asked, not being able to see through the burlap sacks and knowing that craw-fishing had its ups and downs.

"We did well, old friend, we did well. In fact I was hoping to trade some, would it be ok to leave a sack or two with you?" Papa asked his friend, already knowing the answer.

"May sure, Jean," replied Tee John, just as he had expected. "Put them in a shed over there, they will keep for a day or so."

While Lill Tee's papa and Tee John carried the heavy sacks off crawfish to the shed, Lill Tee took the opportunity to talk Jean Paul into the upcoming adventure.

"Hey Jean Paul," Lill Tee called as he started his approach to Jean Paul. Lill Tee knew he could not just come out and say, "Let's go get some Swamp Witch Figs." Jean Paul would have taken off so fast there would have been no catching him. Lill Tee knew he had to ease him into it. Almost to a point of cornering him.

"You up for an adventure?" Lill Tee asked his plump friend.

"What kind of adventure?" Jean Paul asked cautiously. He and Lill Tee had been on countless adventures together, and it seemed no matter what the other one got into, they were in it together. Jean Paul questioned his friend, not wanting to commit himself too early.

"I need to get a pail of figs," Lill Tee explained.

John Paul snickered, "That's not an adventure!" he exclaimed, "We got plenty, look around you." Jean Paul was right in what he said, his family did have several fig trees.

"You're right Jean Paul, but these are no ordinary figs." Lill Tee paused for moment allowing John Paul's curiosity to peak before continuing. "I hear tell they grow the size of your fist, and are so juicy your mouth waters before you take a bite." Lill Tee could see the wheels turning inside Jean Paul's head, if there was one thing Jean Paul liked to do more than anything else, it was eating. The fact that he liked figs just as much as Lill Tee did not did not hurt.

"Wow!" Jean Paul burst out, barely able to contain his excitement, obviously displaying the need to get a hold of some.

"Do you have any like that?" Lill Tee asked, already knowing the answer.

"May no, Lill Tee you know we don't, I don't know anyone who does?" stated Jean Paul, more suspicious now as to where Lill Tee was going with this.

"I think I do," said Lill Tee, beginning to explain. "I hear tell figs grow this big in Devil's Swamp!" Lill tee explained in a calm soft reassuring voice.

"Devil's Swamp!" Jean Paul repeated Lill Tee's words in a calm soft reassuring tone. "ARE

SWAMP WITCH

YOU CRAZY!" Jean Paul called out almost loud enough for their papas to hear. Once again composing himself from the initial shock, he began to respond to Lill Tee's obvious lack of memory.

"Lill Tee, they got a Witch that lives in that swamp!" Jean Paul said, thinking this alone would be all he had to say to remind his friend.

"Now, Jean Paul," Lill Tee said softly, having anticipated his friend's response he was ready. "We're twelve years old, Jean Paul, don't you think we're too old to believe in them kid stories?" Lill Tee finished.

Jean Paul paused for a long while, Lill Tee could almost hear the wheels turning inside of Jean Paul's head, looking for a way out. Then with a hesitant tone, he finally found his tongue.

"I didn't say I believed it, I only said that's what I hear," Jean Paul came back, trying to save face.

Lill Tee knew he had his friend at this point. When you're twelve, you don't want anyone to know you're scared of anything, and you convince yourself you can do anything. "I got him!" Lill Tee thought, "I shamed him just enough to deny his fear of Devil's Swamp. A little more and I could get him to come," Lill Tee reasoned.

"Yea, I know what you mean, Jean Paul," Lill Tee began looking for the knockout punch. "I hear them stories too, stories made up by old people to scare us from going too far into the swamp. I think you and I should be the first to go back there," Lill Tee concluded, still seeing the fear in his friend's face.

"I don't know, Lill Tee," John Paul said, continuing to search for a way to get out of the situation, which had so rapidly developed before he knew what had happened. Pulling him slowly at first then pulling much faster toward his ultimate fate.

"I don't think Papa would let me stay more than one night in the swamp again," said Jean Paul thinking he had found his way out. "I've been away a good bit last couple weeks."

"Is that the only problem?" Lill Tee asked, setting the trap for his reluctant friend.

Jean Paul couldn't think of any other excuse. Normally, saying his papa or mama didn't want him to do something had been plenty enough reason in the past, but for some reason, this time it wasn't. Jean Paul suspected something was up, but he couldn't figure out what. Whatever it was, it was too late now. John Paul had painted himself into a corner, not having any other available exits.

"Yea," Jean Paul finally responded "That's the only reason, why?"

"Because we won't have to stay more than one night in the swamp, we'll be home the next afternoon," Lill Tee reported to his cornered companion.

"Can't be!" Jean Paul contradicted, not willing to go down easy. "The journey will take at least three days paddling alone."

"You're right again, Jean Paul," said Lill

Tee, agreeing with his friend, but continuing to keep his friend off balance. "But we're not going by bayou. I know a short cut over land. Half a day's walk, we're there. Papa showed it to me once when we were trapping out that way. Looking it up on Papa's map, it's not that far by foot."

"But the swamp!" Jean Paul said, his tone starting to sound pleading.

"The water's down and the hard bottom should be dry by now." Lill Tee said, seeing Jean Paul's defiance slowly melting away

"But?" Jean Paul wanted to offer more resistance, but he couldn't think of anything else.

Jean Paul recalled all the favors Lill Tee had done for him, and how no matter what, he would have come through for him. John Paul could hear the determination in Lill Tee's voice and tone. He had seen it many times before, and he knew if he didn't go with him, he would go alone. Jean Paul thought of what might happen if he let

Lill Tee go by himself. As all these thoughts raced through Jean Paul's head, he realized that something happening to his little buddy when he could have been there, was not something he could live with.

"Well, all right!" Jean Paul finally relented, "I'll go."

"Great!" Lill Tee said, the excitement evident in his voice. "Thank you for volunteering."

Jean Paul shot a defiant glance toward Lill Tee. Though not saying a word, Lill Tee understood its meaning.

About this time, their papas walked to where the two boys were sitting on the dock.

"You ready, Lill Tee?" his papa asked, as he hopped into the skiff.

"Yea, Papa," Lill Tee replied, but needed to get one more confirmation about tomorrow, if not from John Paul, maybe from his dad.

"Jean Paul and I was thinking about going do some camping, if it's ok with yall," Lill Tee knew if he got Tee John's OK with the idea, it would be much harder for Jean Paul to change his mind. Besides, this was too important to be left to chance.

"Sure, Lill Tee, I'm a gonna take the crawfish to the store. I won't be needing you," Lill Tee's papa responded as expected, he anxiously waited for Jean Paul's papa to respond.

As Lill Tee looked over to Jean Paul, he looked as though he was frozen, not able to speak. Maybe Jean Paul could have headed it off if only he had found the words sooner. Having relinquished the opportunity to speak first, Jean Paul's papa stepped up to the plate.

"We're almost done, son," Tee John said, rubbing his hand on his son's uncombed head. "You and Lill Tee go pass a good time, you deserve it."

Jean Paul was pale, his last ace in the hole, his dad, had failed to alter his eminent fate.

Lill Tee couldn't help but smile as he called out, "See ya tomorrow, Jean Paul," as he and his papa began rowing away. "Jean Paul is such a chicken," Lill Tee thought, but then he paused for a moment as he began to question his own bravery...... or stupidity. Lill Tee had never been in that part of the swamp before. He had been all around it, but never beyond clearly defined borders. He wanted to ask his papa about Devil's Swamp, but he knew it would only arouse the suspicion of his papa. He knew Papa would not approve of him venturing out so far. So Lill Tee remained silent. As thoughts raced through his mind about the adventure he and Jean Paul was about to embark upon, he once again began playing scenario after scenario in his head of all the possible mishaps that could befall him and his friend, and then he came up with the precautions to eliminate them.

As Lill Tee paddled home with his papa, he found it surprisingly easy to think of dozens of reasons why he should not go to Devil's Swamp. Then Lill Tee thought of his mama and her birthday. There was nothing at this point in his short life he wanted more than to see the look on

SWAMP WITCH

Mama's face when he brought her a big sack of figs. This image in is mind's eye of an event that had not yet happened was what was driving Lill Tee. Enveloping him with the courage and determination he would eventually need to journey into the unknown.

"But hey," Lill Tee thought, "My ancestors had been doing this for years. Way back to the time they came from France and settled up in Canada, some place called Nova Scotia. They didn't know the place, yet they braved the unknown. When we Cajuns were sent away from our new home for not taking the protestant religion, we once again ventured into the unknown to settle here in Louisiana. A land of plenty, a land of beauty and mystery. It's in my blood!" Lill Tee surmised, "I was born to be an adventurer." Lill Tee mused all the way home about how he compared himself to his ancestors.

Upon reaching the dock, Mama and Cotile were waiting. Smoke from the freshly lit fire coiled its way upward slowly dissipating as it made its way toward the sky until it finally tapered off to nothing.

"We got the fire started!" yelled Cotile, as Lill Tee and Papa pulled up to the dock.

The large blackened cast iron pot, which measured approximately four feet across and resembled a soldier's helmet turned upside, now stood ready to receive the catch of the day. Mounted directly on the ground, wood was stacked around it, until the liquid-filled pot was brought to a boil. Steam slowly rising with an occasional splash slipping over the pot's rim indicated the water was now ready. Not to mention the smell of seasoning covering the surrounding area.

Lill Tee and Papa unloaded some of the crawfish, bringing it over to the boiling water. The smell of heavy seasoning rushed into Lill Tee's nostrils, making his eyes water, and causing him to sneeze. "There's no such thing as over-seasoning the water," Lill Tee knew, the more spices the better.

SWAMP WITCH

Lill Tee could only watch as Papa emptied the sack, lifting it effortless into the pot, dumping its contents in the water. Papa shook the sack trying to shake free any remaining crawfish that may have clung to the burlap sack in an effort to delay their final fate. The crawfish moved violently for only a moment before the boiling water quickly transformed their once dull, brownish red hull to bright red.

Lill Tee's mama stood ready with an old boat paddle, using the edge of the pot as a lever, Mama stuck the paddle down into the boiling water then pulled back on the handle. This, "rolled the pot," pulling the crawfish from the bottom where the vat was the hottest to the top and vice versa. This was done quickly and deliberately, because of the intense heat from all sides of the pot, it would not take long to get burned.

The anticipation of the mouth-watering crawfish made the ten-minute boil seem much longer. But before long, Lill Tee's papa had his net and began scooping the mudbugs into large pans, which waited nearby.

A feast by anyone's standards was a table full of crawfish seasoned just right. The peppered spices would slightly sting your mouth and burn your lips. Somewhere between pleasure and pain lies the secret Cajun seasoning, and Lill Tee's mama had developed it to a fine art form.

It did not take long for the enormous pile of crawfish to be transformed to a pile of hulls. Hollowed out carcasses of crawfish covered the table with the size of the piles directly corresponding to the speed of the peeler. Papa's pile was by far the biggest. This is not to say he ate the most, just peeled the most. Eating only every third one, he passed the others to Cotile.

After the meal was completed, everyone gathered around the fireplace. Papa would take the moment to smoke his pipe, while Mama brought out the bible for them to practice their reading. Lill Tee envied his sister's reading ability, and appreciated all the help she offered him through the years.

As bedtime once again rolled around, the once-blazing fire dispatched only glowing embers of what once was.

All throughout dinner and the fireside reading, Lill Tee could not escape the thoughts of tomorrow. In his mind, he had taken the journey many times. Back and forth the scenario played though his mind, as the reality of the moment seemed somewhat less clear than the journey.

Anticipation had long since begun to mount as he anxiously waited for morning and what lay ahead. As Lill Tee lay in bed, he could not escape the thoughts and fears of the dangers of his quest. Though vaguely understood, he could not fully appreciate the dangers until ultimately confronted by them face to face. Each time he ran the scenario through his mind, if only subconsciously, he would omit any of the inevitable setbacks or dangers. Each time, the trip went smoothly, without a hitch. Lill Tee, however, had a gut feeling this trip would be anything but routine, or smooth. There was no way for Lill Tee to know that in less than nine hours, he would embark on a journey that would test not only the strength of his resolve, but the strength of a friendship. Images swirling about with different colors and patterns were Lill Tee's thought's, each different, overlapping one another as they slowly twirled in his mind, until he slowly sank into unconsciousness, and drifted off to sleep.

The next morning, Lill Tee awoke anxious, ready to begin his journey, his excitement obvious to everyone around him. The morning fell into place just as he had anticipated. Papa left the dock just as Jean Paul paddled up.

Lill Tee had been ready for quite a while by the time Jean Paul pulled up to the dock, and he did not want to waste any time. Lill Tee tossed a backpack and a coil of rope into the pirogue before climbing in. Then straddling both sides of the small craft, he crawled into position. The backpack contained several biscuits and molasses his mama carefully packed for the trip, and the rope was brought along just in case. Past experience had shown both Jean Paul and Lill Tee the value of being prepared. The two boys paddled out as the sun was just starting to lighten up the surrounding area. Lill Tee and Jean Paul stuck hard to their task, exchanging few words as they paddled, each equally determined to accomplish their goal without mishap.

"You still sure about this, Lill Tee?" Jean Paul questioned his friend, as though to give him one last chance to back out. When in reality, it was Jean Paul who was now questioning the intelligence of their decision.

"You bet ya!" Lill Tee said, leaning into the paddle, pulling the pirogue forward. "You not having second thoughts, are you?" Lill Tee asked, a broad unseen smile on his face.

"Not me!" Jean Paul quickly replied, "You know me, I'm always up for adventure."

Lill Tee laughed inside, he knew his friend

was nervous, but he also knew he would see it through to the end.

After several hours of paddling, the two boys began to emerge from the cypress trees and into areas that were vastly more open. Razor grass replaced tall trees, allowing them to see far greater distance in every direction. Arriving at the first leg of their journey, they had made better time than Lill Tee had anticipated, beating the morning sun, as it just now began to make it' presence known over the cypress trees. The heat of the sun felt good, since the early morning had been rather chilly close to the water in their tiny craft.

The boys steered the pirogue to a small indention on the bank that could easily accommodate the size of their craft. The boys surged forward as the craft ran into the bank.

Lill Tee climbed out the front of the pirogue, then pulled the bow onto the bank.

"Get the rope," Lill Tee reminded Jean Paul as he began to work his way onto land.

SWAMP WITCH

"Catch!" Jean Paul said, as he tossed Lill Tee the backpack, and then the rope. Jean Paul, slowly stepped out of the pirogue, cautious so as not to fall. He knew it would not be a happy day for him if he were soaking wet. Pulling the pirogue a few yards into the razor grass, it essentially hid it, as the razor grass was taller than the side of the pirogue.

"See the oaks in that tree line on the horizon?" Lill Tee asked, pointing in the direction of the trees.

"Wow!" Jean Paul said, indicating his surprise. "That seems like it's way over there."

"Well, you know how we're going to get there, don't you?" Lill asked, picking up the backpack and handing Jean Paul the rope.

"How?" Jean Paul asked, wondering if Lill Tee had a surprise up his sleeve.

"Walk!" Lill Tee jokily responded, as he began to walk away.

"Walk," Jean Paul said under his breath, not finding Lill Tee's joke nearly as funny as Lill

SWAMP WITCH

Tee had found it.

As Jean Paul caught up, Lill Tee turned and called back to Jean Paul as he continued to walk.

"Going over land, we should be able to cut about a day's paddling," Lill Tee said, trying to motivate his friend. "The only other way to get to Devil's Swamp is to travel upstream, where a small bayou branches off leading into the swamp," Lill concluded his explanation for the purpose of keeping Jean Paul as informed as possible. Lill Tee knew if this trip were to be a success, they would both have to be on the same page and working together as a team.

The swamp, by itself, was a formidable place with poisonous snakes, wild animals and if that wasn't enough, the occasional patch of quicksand. Many a Cajun had gone into Devil's Swamp and never returned.

Legend has it, a Witch guards over Devil's Swamp. A Witch who has been doomed by the Devil himself to guard over his namesake.

SWAMP WITCH

Legend also has it that plants grow to a tremendous size and this is what the two young adventurers sought, tremendous figs. Because your typical fig tree is not actually a tree at all, but a rather large bush that grows a tantalizing fruit, which is always a welcomed treat, but to have figs like the ones described in Devil's Swamp would indeed be a special treat.

The morning progressed slowly, as Jean Paul and Lill Tee walked through the razor grass, which was continually changing in height and thickness. Although the tree line did not appear to be getting closer, they knew each step brought them that much closer to the tree line, and their ultimate goal.

As the redundancy of the trek continued, they began to become less aware of the surroundings that never seemed to change. This would prove to be a near-fatal error, as Lill Tee stepped through the razor grass and into a small opening.

Lill Tee knew he should stop, but the

opening had appeared so quickly and without warning, his momentum had brought him forward.

"Ahhhh!" Lill Tee yelled the only sound he was able to get out before falling into the quicksand. Lill Tee felt himself sink, he knew not to struggle for that would only draw him down more.

"Jean Paul!" Lill Tee yelled, "Watch out! It's quicksand!"

Seconds later, Jean Paul slowly emerged from the razor grass. Peering into the opening, Jean Paul saw Lill Tee up to his neck in the quicksand bog.

Pulling the rope off his neck, Jean Paul found the end and tossed the rest of the coil to Lill Tee.

Lill Tee had continued to sink with the bog up to his chin. He reached for the rope, but could not reach it. Jean Paul saw the problem and retrieved the rope and cast it out once again, this time landing within Lill Tee's grasp.

SWAMP WITCH

Grabbing the rope, Lill Tee made a series of quick wraps around his hand then told Jean Paul, "Pull!"

Jean Paul leaned against the rope, pushing using the entire weight of his body to pull his friend to safety. At first, it looked as though his effort would be futile as the bog had too great a suction on him. Any progress Jean Paul made was quickly reclaimed by the bog and brought Lill Tee even farther into the bog, until Lill Tee's head became completely submerged. Refusing to admit defeat, and knowing his friend's life hung in the balance, Jean Paul pulled, pulled as though he had somehow become processed. The rope tightened to a point Jean Paul thought it would snap, but it held and slowly at first, then more gradually, Lill Tee began to break the surface of the bog on his way to freedom.

Lill Tee gasped for air as his friend continued to pull him to safety. Reaching the safety of the razor grass, Lill Tee and Jean Paul collapsed with exhaustion.

SWAMP WITCH

Gradually regaining both their strength and composure, the two boys rose to their feet.

"Thanks pal!" Lill Tee said, as he hugged his plump friend. "You saved my life!"

"I didn't do anything you would not have done," Jean Paul responded, still winded from his ordeal.

"You need a rest?" Lill Tee asked, seeing how hard his friend was breathing.

"No, I'll be alright, let's keep moving," Jean Paul said, gathering up the rope.

The progress throughout the rest of the morning was a little slower, more cautious, for obvious reasons. But eventually they arrived at the tree line, which was Devil's Swamp.

Ironically, it was not until this point that Lill Tee began to question his resolve.

"What if the stories are true?" he pondered, as he trudged through the grass. "What if a Witch does live there? Would she cast a spell on us, or worse?" Lill Tee questioned, still moving steadily forward. The unknown was always uncertain, and growing up as a young Cajun, you craved to explore. Going farther and farther, seeking new territory, if only new to you. For this reason, many of the old Cajun stories, were designed to establish a border in which their young could begin to develop the skills needed to survive in the swamp, and still establish a safety for them in the event something would happen.

It was noon before Jean Paul and Lill Tee eventually settled down for a little lunch. Pulling the backpack from his back, Lill Tee set it on a log.

"Good thing Mama packed the food good," Lill Tee said, referring to how wet everything had gotten when he went in the quick sand.

He served the contents of his backpack to his anxious friend, who gave every indication he was about to die from starvation. If there was one thing Jean Paul seldom missed, that was a meal.

The rest was sorely needed, for the two boys were both exhausted. Lill Tee had severely underestimated the difficulty of the journey or time it would take. He thought they were about half way, and he now knew they would not make it out of the swamp tonight. Even if they turned back now, they would never make it out on time.

But Lill Tee chose not to share this thought with Jean Paul, for he knew he disliked being in the swamp after dark. They had hoped to camp on some high ground, but they were not quite there yet. "Besides, why get Jean Paul excited and discontent before it was time," Lill Tee thought.

"How much farther?" Jean Paul asked, as though somehow reading Lill Tee's mind.

"Not much," Lill Tee replied, deceiving his gullible friend.

After resting for a while, they found renewed strength and forged on. At this point, Lill Tee was being led by only his instincts, not having definite boundaries or landmarks to rely on. Jean Paul never questioned Lill Tee's judgment until toward the end of the day when the sun started setting, and the swamp started to darken. Shadows began to form as the light disappeared, taking with it the last remnant of light.

At this point, Lill Tee really began to worry. He had thought he would be in and out of the swamp by now, but his determination led him to lose all track of time.

"We need to find some high ground," Lill Tee told Jean Paul, trying to keep as upbeat and confident as possible.

But Jean Paul knew as well as Lill Tee that the swamp was unforgiving.

The two boys struggled through the darkness, unable to see but a short distance away, their hearts grew heavy; adding to the emotional distress was the physical torment of mosquitoes. They grow big in the swamp, covering the exposed limbs and face of the two young boys as they trekked forward.

Each mosquito took its turn sucking the blood from their skin. They didn't swat them though, for they knew that would only bring more. The smell of blood would attract them like a magnet, so the two boys merely suffered in silence.

The moon rose early in its full amber glow. This helped lighten up the swamp and they found travel less difficult.

A glimpse of light in the far distance, then gone again! Was it a light at all? Or was Lill Tee's eyes playing tricks on him? Not knowing the answer, and having no other firm direction, Lill Tee headed in the direction of the light.

As they drew closer, the light became visible once more, and grew brighter with each step. They were well into the tree line now, and the ground began a gradual incline until finally they were on high ground again.

Lill Tee peered into the distance, he saw several fig trees, each were the size of small trees. Their branches weighed down by the enormous fruit that hung on it.

"They are huge!" Lill Tee thought, catching

SWAMP WITCH

his breath. "Have you ever seen figs this big?" Lill Tee asked Jean Paul, who was stretched out beside him, hardly even noticing the trees.

They were not the size of your fist, like Lill Tee had reported, but they were bigger than any he had ever seen.

"No way!" Jean Paul called out; his eyes fixed on the prize they had sought.

But beyond the trees lay the house, the house both of them had heard stories about. It was nothing more than a run down shack made from cypress nailed in a vertical position. The window shutters were open and a cotton mesh took the place of windows, providing only partial protection against mosquitoes. The porch was small, just big enough for one rocking chair, to the side of the door.

"But a Witch doesn't need much room, she doesn't get much company," Lill Tee thought he could see a shadow moving within the house, and they knew she was home.

A chill ran through them. "Let's get our figs

and get out of here!" Lill Tee told Jean Paul.

The two boys worked quickly, perhaps a little carelessly. It was not clear what was the culprit that finally gave them away, if it the squashing wet shoes or their movement that caught the Witch's eye.

But caught is what they were. Lill Tee never saw her come out on the porch, he never heard her come out. A flash of light and a loud blast from a shotgun sent both Jean Paul and Lill Tee sprawling face down to the ground.

"Who goes there!" she yelled, in a voice that pieced the darkness, and their souls.

"I'm dead!" Lill Tee thought, "The witch is going to kill me." Still in shock and half frozen with fear, Lill Tee found it within himself to answer.

"My name's Lill Tee!" he yelled, not knowing if calling out was the right thing to do.

"Show yourself!" she demanded.

Lill Tee rose on his trembling legs and walked over to her. Her face was partially concealed by the cabin light and he could just make out her features. She was a big woman for these parts. Her lined and wrinkled face showed her years. She had short gray hair, which hung, although thinning as it reached the top of her head. Her recessed lips indicated her teeth had left her, and with all the outward signs of this old woman, the one that got Lill Tee's attention the most was the fact that she held a double-barreled shotgun.

As Lill Tee approached and came into the light, her facial expression changed from a snarl to a look of surprise.

"Why you just a boy!" she said, as the barrel of her gun started to lower. Then as though she caught herself, she pulled it back up and pointed it at Jean Paul, who was still sprawled out on the ground. "And what's that other lump of flesh over yonder!" she demanded.

"That's my friend, Jean Paul, Jean Paul come here!" said Lill Tee in an excited voice.

Jean Paul jumped to his feet and ran next

to Lill Tee. Seeing Jean Paul was a boy also, she lowered her shotgun.

"What you boys doing out here!" she demanded, her tone meaning business.

"We was, ..we ah?" Lill Tee was dumfounded, how could he tell this person, who was probably going to kill them anyway, that they came all this way to steal from her figs.

As he pondered his response, it proved unnecessary as she noticed the spilled sack of figs.

"Well, I see I got fig thieves here! I could shoot you and be in my rights!" she yelled, as they stood as motionless as two trembling boys could.

Apparently seeing how scared they were, her heart must have softened a bit. She began to take a softer tone toward them.

"Your parents never taught you about stealing? Why didn't you ask for figs?" she asked, "There's enough trees around here for you to have plenty."

SWAMP WITCH

Not quite understanding the softness in her tone, Lill Tee cautiously answered her.

"We were scared,"

"Scared to ask an old Witch for the figs?" she questioned.

Lill Tee and John Paul looked at each other, amazed she confessed to what they had already suspected. Mistaking her statement for being a confirmation of what they had already suspected, she actually affirmed to them what she was. The two boys grew even more scared than they were before, and perhaps seeing their shaken expressions, she decided to ease their troubled minds.

"Relax boys, I'm not a Witch. I was just repeating what the folks round here say about me," said the old woman in a more relaxed tone.

It felt as though a weight had been lifted from Lill Tee and Jean Paul.

"You boys come in and dry yourself by the fire," said the old lady, in a soft tone.

The two boys were reluctant at first, but

then reasoned that if she wanted to kill them, she would have done it by now.

The inside of the cabin was a simple one-room building, with a table, chair, bed, and a rocking chair, inventorying the whole cabin.

"How you boys got all the way out here?" she asked, apparently not used to seeing too many people.

"We paddled some, and walked the rest," Lill Tee replied, starting to feel more at ease with the old woman.

"You come a long way to steal figs," she asked, still not having a clear understanding of the two boys' motivation.

"We heard you had the biggest around," Lill Tee offered, "I wanted to get some for my mother's birthday tomorrow, I thought they would make an excellent present."

"Where did you land your pirogue?" she asked?

"By Birdman's Cove," Lill Tee replied without hesitation.

SWAMP WITCH

"That's a half day ride!" the old lady replied, somewhat taken back by their answer. She eyed the two boys hard once more as though not believing they could make such a journey through the swamp.

"Well, that was the shortest way," he replied. "By boat, it's almost a day paddling if you don't have a motor."

As they talked, Lill Tee began to sense kindness in her voice, softness in her only partially masked by harshness. As Lill Tee sat there looking at her, she reached into her pocket and pulled out a corncob pipe. Reaching for a jar of tobacco she had handy, she packed the pipe, and then lit it. Soon, swirls of white smoke encircled her as she puffed on the pipe, pausing momentarily to contemplate her thoughts before finally speaking once more.

"Your folks know were you are?" she finally asked.

"They think we're camping," Lill Tee responded, questioning whether or not he should divulge too much information.

"Don't get many folks out this way anymore," said the old lady with an almost undetectable sigh.

"Why do they say you're a Witch?" Lill Tee asked as if a sudden surge of courage had just swept through him. She eyed Lill Tee hard, before finally answering him.

"Rumor spreads like wild fire in the swamp," she said. "People takes what they hear and add to it, pretty soon you can't tell the truth from a lie. I wasn't always alone out here," she began to explain. "I was married to a local Indian. A good man. We were married for many years. As he was dying, he requested I give him a ritual burial. A ceremony he had gone over with me till I had it memorized. Upon his death, I began the ceremony. It would last an entire day, involve fire dancing and chants. During the ceremony, I caught a man looking on, in this most private time of grief. I chased him off, I'm sure he's the one who started the rumor. It don't matter no way, I'm an old woman and got no use for many people. What were you boys going to do tonight?" she asked, wondering how they would make it all night outside without a fire.

"We were going to find some high ground and build a fire," said Lill Tee.

"High ground!" she said, with a laugh. "There is none, you're sitting on the only acre of high ground between us and your pirogue. Pass the night on the floor and in the morning, if you still want them figs, I'll give you a chance to work for them."

"What kind of work?" Lill Tee asked, then catching himself after realizing that it didn't really matter.

"In the morning," the old lady said, and then blew out the lantern, lying back on her moss mattress.

The cabin took on an eerie silence, the sounds of wildlife penetrated the cabin till Tee lay there with Jean Paul, who was unable to find anything to say since the old lady had surprised them with her shotgun. Jean Paul now lay snoring in a dead sleep.

Lill Tee listened; he tried to attach an animal to each sound he heard. The sound of tiny paws splashing one and then the other into the water probably belonged to a raccoon looking for a meal. The distinctive sound air makes as it is forced through features probably belonged to an owl out on the prowl. Frogs, mosquitoes, and the list went on until Lill Fee finally drifted off to sleep.

Jean Paul and Lill Tee awoke the next morning to the smell of fried corn meal.

"You boys get a glass, come get some cush cush," the old woman directed, stirring the pot over the stove. Cush cush was a common meal among bayou folk. It consisted of fried corn meal and milk, joined together to form a liquid mash of sorts.

After downing their cush cush, the boys followed the old woman outside.

"The area takes on a much different

appearance during the day," Lill Tee thought, as he began to scan the area for landmarks he found last night. Further down was an orchard of orange and apple trees, which he had not seen. Also escaping their view on either side of the hill, which probably ran for a hundred yards, was a small barn of sorts with various sounds that could be heard, but not seen at this point.

They followed the old lady to a pile of wood, which had been cut but not split.

"You boys split my wood and I give you figs, and a ride to your pirogue," she said, eyeing the two boys hard.

"Is it a deal?"

Lill Tee and Jean Paul immediately shook their heads in rapid unison, for the first time causing the old woman to smile, in as much as a toothless woman can.

She then turned away, leaving the boys to their work. Lill Tee turned to Jean Paul, who had still not spoken since yesterday.

"Can you still talk, Jean Paul?" he asked.

SWAMP WITCH

His chubby friend mumbled to Lill Tee.

"I can talk, but let's get this wood split so we can get out of here!" Jean Paul responded, a nervous tone in his voice.

Lill Tee had become somewhat at ease with the old woman, but Jean Paul had remained suspicious of her. The boys talked for several minutes, but Lill Tee could say nothing to him that would change his mind. For the better part of the morning, they split wood. The morning sun was hot and before long, they were wet with sweat, but they stayed to their task.

The old woman came out of her shack with a bundle under her arms and two large sacks in each hand.

"Let's go boys, time to get yall back," The old woman said, as she began walking off, not looking to see if the boys were following or not.

They followed her to a skiff, which had been partially pulled on the bank. Both the boys' breathed a sign of relief when they saw it had a motor on it. Their arms and backs were sore from cutting wood; they didn't want to paddle all afternoon too.

Lill Tee and John Paul sat on the middle bench as she maneuvered her way through the maze of bayous, which Lill Tee had long since stopped trying to remember. Finding her way through each turn with confidence, riding in an area she called her back yard. After several hours, the old woman pulled along side Jean Paul's pirogue.

"You boys don't forget them figs now," the old woman said, as they started to get out the skiff.

"Thanks a lot," Lill Tee said as he waved.

"You boys are welcome back," she said "but next time, come during the day," the old woman said, her toothless smile showing once more, as the skiff putted out of sight.

Lill Tee and Jean Paul readied the pirogue for the long ride home.

"Phew!" Jean Paul said, as they paddled along the bayou. "I was never so scared all my life!" said Jean Paul. "Hey Lill Tee, next time you get a big idea, don't think of me, OK!"

Lill Tee knew Jean Paul didn't mean it for the next time Lill Tee would embark on an adventure, he knew Jean Paul would be right by his side.

The early afternoon sun beat down on the two young adventures as they paddled for home. With virtually no wind ,a dead calm had settled over the bayou, its glass-like appearance made paddling much easier and they made good time, finally arriving at Lill Tee's house. As they paddled around the bend in the bayou, they could see Cotile sitting on the dock, waiting for them.

"Lill Tee!" she shouted, getting everyone's attention. Pulling up to the dock, Lill Tee handed one of the sacks to Cotile.

"Whatcha got in them sacks?" Curiosity getting the best of her.

"Cotile," Lill Tee said, "you bring this sack to Mama and tell her happy birthday from both of us."

Cotile had a puzzled look on her face, but followed her brother's instructions. Lill Tee watched at a distance, wanting to see Mama's face as she opened the sack to find the biggest plumpish figs she ever laid her eyes on. The look on her face and the joy in her eyes was worth every mosquito bite and every sore muscle he had to endure during the trip.

Papa also smiled, knowing what he had to go through to get those figs, better than Mama did. A smile of pride came over him as if he was just now starting to realize Lill Tee was becoming a man.

As for Jean Paul, he wasted no time hanging around. He got in his pirogue and pushed away from the dock.

"See Ya, Lill Tee!" Jean Paul called out, pushing away from the dock. "Next time you get a big idea for an adventure, don't think of Jean Paul, OK."

Lill Tee just smiled and waved farewell to

his faithful friend. In the years that followed, Lill Tee made several more trips to the old woman's cabin, whose name he later would find out to be Norma Fitch. Over time, they became friends and Norma became much less of a recluse. As word spread, more people would stop by to talk and trade with the one-time legendary Witch. By the time she left this world, she had become one of the most-liked people on the bayou.

With all the subsequent trips Lill Tee and Papa made to Norma Fitch, none ever would come close to the time he and Jean Paul braved the unknown to face their fear and came face to face with the SWAMP WITCH!